THE
MU LAN CHUAN
EXERCISE BOOK

Eight Techniques for Better Health

SHENG KENG YUN

SAMUEL WEISER, INC.
York Beach, Maine

First published in 1998 by
SAMUEL WEISER, INC.
Box 612
York Beach, ME 03910-0612

Library of Congress Cataloging-in-Publication Data

Sheng, Keng Yun.
    Mu Lan Chuan exercise book : eight techniques for
better health / Sheng Keng Yun.
        p. cm.
    Includes index.
    ISBN 1-57863-049-5 (alk. paper)
    1. Mu-lan ch'üan. 2. Health. I. Title.
GV505.S547 1998
613.7'1--dc21   98-7468
                                                      CIP

MG
Typeset in 11.5 Truesdell
Cover and text design by Kathryn Sky-Peck

Printed in the United States of America

05 04 03 02 01 00 99 98
10 9 8 7 6 5 4 3 2 1

The paper used in this publication meets all the minimum requirements of the
American National Standard for Permanence of Paper for
Printed Library Materials Z39.48.1984.

To the memory of my father and mother. My father, who was a Taoist, inspired me to study Chi Kung and Tai Chi Chuan when I was very young. He often brought me to watch martial arts, Tai Chi Chuan, when I was about 6 years old, and I loved Chi Kung and Tai Chi Chuan. My mother was a Buddhist and a vegetarian. Both parents always taught me to be kind to people, to help people when they face difficulties, and to do beneficial things for people as much as possible. I have endeavored always to act according to my parents' instruction.

Women hold up half the sky.

Knowing satisfaction will always make you happy.

A WOMAN RIDES A GALLANT HORSE, while I ride on an ugly donkey. Looking forward at her, it seems that I am not as rich as she. When I look backward, I see a man pushing a wheelbarrow. Comparatively speaking, when I look forward, I am not so wealthy as she, but looking backward, I am rich enough and feel very lucky and comfortable.

❖

WHEN YOU MEET YOUR MOST INTIMATE FRIEND, you would like to drink one thousand cups of wine with this person, but you will think it is not enough. But when you don't want to talk with someone, you will think a half sentence is too much to waste.

Contents

CONTENTS

To Miss Sheng Keng Yun

Your potential talent and noble character

are just like

a most transparent jade

with a cover

This precious jade was hidden in the Jing Mountain.

Your future

is brilliant,

Having no known limits.

At the Year of the Horse

in San Francisco

—Yan Xin

Preface

THE LEGEND OF MU LAN is based on a Southern and Northern Dynasty (420–589) narrative poem called "The Song of Mu Lan." I love this song. It tells the story of Mu Lan when she left her family. On the way to the battlefield, she missed her parents, her younger brother and sister, and her hometown. When I studied in primary and middle schools, we could hear "The Song of Mu Lan" everywhere, because everybody loved to sing it, including me. All Chinese people admired the fact that Mu Lan went off into the battlefield in place of her sick and old father. After fearless fighting in many battles for twelve years, she accomplished many wonderful heroic deeds; she was awarded many honors and was offered a high position. At last Mu Lan returned home, a glorious heroine.

I compiled Mu Lan Chuan according to Mu Lan's movements, which I practiced when I was very young. The movements of Mu Lan Chuan are very graceful and beautiful. Most of the movements use the whole body and stimulate important acupuncture points, which I discuss later in the book.

In China, the story of Mu Lan is a well-known and well-loved fairy tale. Hua Mu Lan was born in Yenan City in Shensi

*Hua Mu Lan departing from her aged parents
and little brother for the battlefield.*

Province in the southeast of China, a famous place known for its revolutionary activities. It is also known as a holy place. Mu Lan's hometown was near Wan Hua Shan ("Ten Thousand Flowers Mountain"), and Wan Hua Shan is one of the most scenic and beautiful places in the country. Every afternoon, Hua Mu Lan practiced her exercises to improve her skills.

Mu Lan was an obedient girl. She loved her parents, and her parents loved her. Above all, she loved her country. She was the eldest, and had a younger brother and sister. Every day, at the break of the day, when the rooster crowed, she quickly jumped up from bed and went to her weaving room and sat in front of the loom to weave cloth until noon. She worked very diligently every day.

In the afternoon, she went to Wan Hua Shan with her father to practice her exercises. Her father, Hua Hoo, was a famous general in the army, and his skill was known throughout the entire country. Day by day she learned from her father. Her father noticed how well his daughter was doing. Mu Lan was clever and very diligent in everything she did. She exercised very seriously and learned every skill from her father. She could quickly understand and master everything he taught her, so her father decided to teach her all he knew. He also taught her the special techniques he used on the battlefield. Because Hua Mu Lan was so ambitious, she wanted to learn from her father all that he knew and she was driven to try to become as much of a master as he was.

It is said that more than one thousand and three hundred years ago, the enemy invaded China. The old battlefield was near Mongolia. The Chinese Emperor ordered Hua Mu Lan's father to fight the enemy. At that time, her father was sick and too weak to fight. He was ashamed to say that he was unable to fight, and he feared that if he did not obey the order of the emperor, he would be punished by death.

Facing such a miserable condition, how could Mu Lan afford to see her beloved father die? In her mind Mu Lan thought: my father has taught me all he knows about the art of warfare, and I have learned many special techniques to defeat the enemy on the battlefield. At last she decided to go to the battlefield to fight the enemy in her father's place.

In the beginning her parents did not want to let her go to the battlefield, but in the end, they found it useless to try to stop her because she was so determined to save her father and her country.

Usually Mu Lan was a good daughter. Every other time she had listened to her parents and done as they had ordered her to do. This time no one could convince her, no one could prevent her or change her mind. She made a decision and felt she must abide by it. She would not change her mind by argument or by reason. In her inner heart, her decision was based on her love for her parents, her family, and her country.

At last she decided upon a plan. She determined that she would pretend to be her father. She cut her hair short, just like a man's. She wore her father's military clothes and long boots, and she also carried his sword and long knife. When it was time for battle, she led her soldiers bravely to the battlefield to fight the enemy.

She was very brave, never thinking of herself, and she was not concerned with preserving her own life. In the battles, she courageously killed many enemy soldiers, and defeated the troops that remained. When she had won her final victory, she returned to report to the Emperor.

When the Emperor heard this victorious news, he was extremely happy. At that time the Emperor was looking for a son-in-law for his beautiful daughter. Seeing Mu Lan as a very smart and handsome general, the Emperor was favorably impressed and wanted Mu Lan to be his son-in-law.

In ancient times, China was a very large country, even as it is now, and communication was not very good. Mu Lan's hometown was far away from the palace where the Emperor lived, so the Emperor did not really know anything about general Mu Lan. The Emperor was finally told that Mu Lan was a maiden girl and could not marry the Emperor's daughter! According to ancient law, Mu Lan had deceived the Emperor, and, therefore, should be punished by death. But because she had defeated the enemy and had done such brilliant and meritorious work for her country, the Emperor let her return to her native town as a glorious heroine. Ever after, millions of Chinese would celebrate her courage in saving their country.

Introduction:
The Benefits of Mu Lan Chuan

MU LAN CHUAN IS VERY GRACEFUL KUNG. The stances are different from any other forms of Tai Chi Chuan and Chi Kung. There are many benefits from doing this kung, because the forms use the whole body and quickly increase your energy. Above all, you should relax and be happy. When you practice Mu Lan Chuan, you will feel stronger and it will not take very long before you notice a change in your energy.

In the first section, you will use the "Crossing Legs" form. You squat and stand and allow your knees to stimulate the acupuncture point called "Chengshan." "Crossing Legs" will help cure low back pain, spasms of the gastrocnemius, hemorrhoids, and constipation.

In the second section, you will work with the feet—the roots of the body. Your feet are the reflexes of all the body's organs, glands, and limbs. When your heels are off the ground, the toes must firmly grasp the ground. In this way, Mu Lan Chuan will improve the condition of your pituitary gland, neck, eyes, ears, lungs, stomach, ureter tube, kidneys, liver, and sciatic nerve.

Next you will use breath to improve your health. When you exhale, you expel stale and waste Chi (air) out of your body. When you inhale, it increases your fresh air and oxygen. Why? Because you use "favorable breathing." How do you do this? During inhaling your diaphragm descends and the abdominal wall protrudes, and reverse movements occur. When you exhale, the abdominal wall is concave. This exercise achieves a greater expansion of diaphragmatic movement. Moving the abdominal wall is a type of abdominal breathing that may help you stay youthful.

In the third section—"The Wind Blowing the Willow"— you beat your buttocks gently with your fists and stimulate the Huantiao acupuncture point. This can help heal pain in your lower back and hip region, muscular atrophy, or any motor impairment, pain, or weakness of the lower extremities (hands and feet); this exercise also helps hemiplegia.

You will also learn "Swinging Hands." As your hands are swinging back and forth, they will touch the Mingmen, an acupuncture point opposite your navel. This activity will stimulate the acupuncture point. "Swinging Hands" alleviates stiffness, lumbago, leukorrhea, impotence, seminal emissions, and diarrhea.

Publisher's Note

THE AUTHOR AND PUBLISHER of this material are not responsible in any manner whatsoever for any injury caused directly or indirectly by reading or following the instructions in this text. The physical and psychological activities described in the text may be too strenuous for some people. Readers of this text should consult a qualified physician before engaging in these, or any other, exercises.

If you have a medical condition, or are of uncertain health, immediately seek attention and advice from a qualified medical doctor. Although the practice of these exercises is beneficial in many instances, they are neither a diagnostic tool nor an exclusive treatment for pathological conditions. These exercises can be used to complement, but not replace, a doctor's care.

CHAPTER 1
THE FIRST TECHNIQUE

Preparing Posture

Stand with your feet parallel and as wide apart as your shoulders (fig. 1). Smile inwardly and outwardly. Allow your body to be relaxed and tranquil, thinking nothing. Rotate your tongue inside your mouth. When there is saliva, swallow it to allow it to sink down to your "Dan Tian," an acupuncture point that is three fingers below your navel. Do this three times.

FIG. 1

A Pair of Eagles Flying

Raise your hands and arms and stretch them to the left and right sides of your body, with palms facing downward (fig. 2). Moving slowly and smoothly, let the palms fall down and lift them up; then repeat again, letting the palms fall down and then lift them up. Repeat these movements nine times. Slowly let both hands fall down to the sides of your body.

FIG. 2

Bowing Politely

Stand quietly; lift up your left or right hand (fig. 3), bending your four fingers, and put your thumb over them, forming a fist. Then, with your left hand embracing the right fist (fig. 4), raise your embracing fists together in front of your head (fig. 5). Slowly and politely bow down and lift up your head three times (fig. 6). Then separate the fists and let them fall down to the sides of your body (fig. 7).

FIG. 3

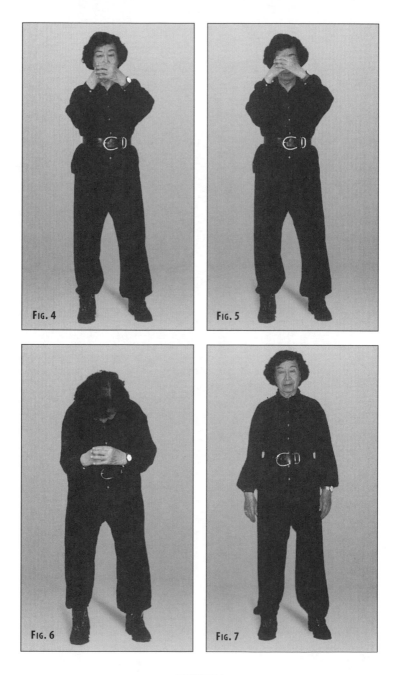

FIG. 4

FIG. 5

FIG. 6

FIG. 7

Forming an Arc

Stand quietly. Feet are parallel, as wide apart as your shoulders (fig. 8). Draw back your right foot one step (fig. 9). Turn your left heel on the ground and turn your toes toward the right side, continuing to turn your body to the right side (fig. 10). Turning 180 degrees, step forward with your right leg and foot, forming an arc. The weight of your body is on the back foot (left foot). Then, like a pair of eagles flying, with palms stretched and facing downward, slowly and happily move your arms and hands up and down nine times (fig. 11).

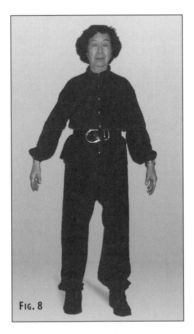

FIG. 8

FIG. 9

Then change, draw back the left foot parallel to the right foot. Stretch arms and hands to sides, and again, draw back the left foot one step. With the heel of the right foot on the ground and toes turning toward the left side, turn your body to the left side, and continue turning to 180 degrees in the opposite direction, with your left leg and foot stepping forward one step, forming an arc. Do this sequence nine times.

Continue to turn your body to the right side, turning 180 degrees (fig. 12). Then step forward, with your right leg and foot forming an arc (fig. 13). The weight of your body is on the left foot, which is to the rear.

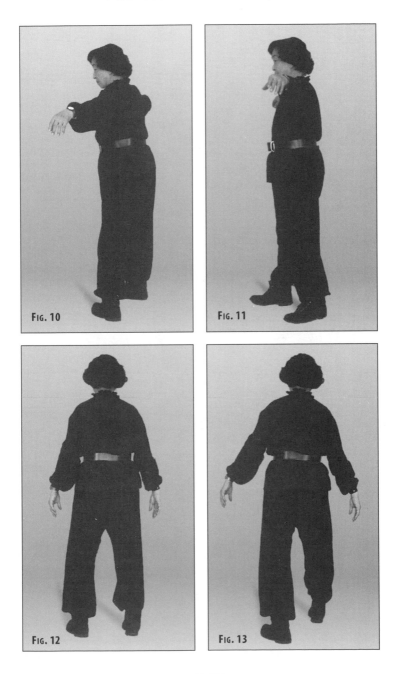

FIG. 10

FIG. 11

FIG. 12

FIG. 13

FIG. 14

FIG. 15

Then like a pair of eagles flying, with palms facing downward (fig. 14), slowly and happily move your arms and hands up and down nine times (fig. 15).

Now change, drawing back your left foot parallel to the right foot (fig. 16). Again, draw back the left foot one step, with the heel of the right foot on the ground and the toes turning toward the left side (fig. 17). Turn your body to the left side.

Fig. 16

Fig. 17

Continue turning 180 degrees in the opposite direction, with the left leg and foot stepping forward one step, forming an arc. Do this nine times as before.

Crossing Legs

Stand quietly with your feet parallel and as wide apart as your shoulders (fig. 18). With your right leg and knee crossing the left leg and knee, lift up your right hand and arm in front of you (fig. 19). At the same time, inhale slowly and deeply.

With the left knee touching the back of the right lower leg (fig. 20), and while the hand and arm are moving down, slowly exhale. During the lowering, also lower the body a little so you are in a squatting position. The left knee should remain

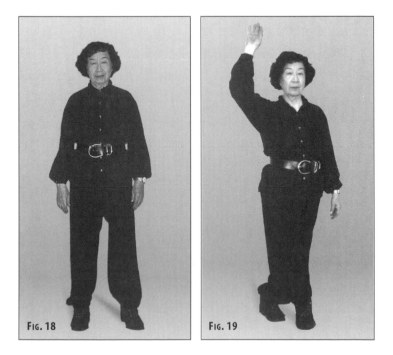

FIG. 18   FIG. 19

FIG. 20

touching the right lower leg. In this way, it can stimulate the important acupuncture point called "Chengshan" (meaning "holding a mountain"). The whole body joins in on these up and down movements. See Diagram 1.

Then change to the left leg and knee, crossing the right leg and knee with the left leg. Lift up your left arm while you do this (fig. 21). Inhale deeply and slowly.

Allow your arm and hand to drop down and exhale slowly (fig. 22). At the same time remember to let your right knee

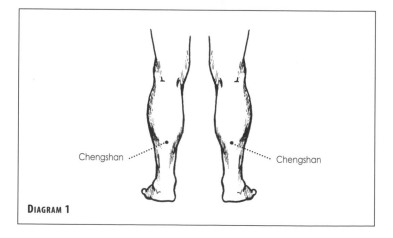

Chengshan ·········· · Chengshan

DIAGRAM 1

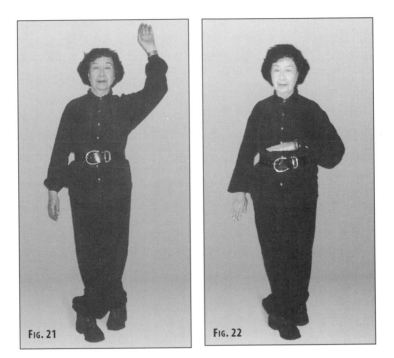

FIG. 21

FIG. 22

touch the left lower leg. This again stimulates the important acupuncture point named "Chengshan." Repeat these movements nine times on each foot. At the beginning, if you cannot do the exercise nine times, you may reduce it to three times.

Moon-like Leg

Stand quietly with your feet parallel and pointing forward. Slowly lift up both arms and stretch your arms outward from both sides of the body to the height of your shoulders (fig. 23).

Bend your hands from the wrist so that your fingers point upward. Straighten your arms, and slowly move the weight of your body onto your right foot. As you stand firmly, raise up your left foot and leg toward the back of your body (fig. 24).

FIG. 23

FIG. 24

Raise up and let your hands fall down nine times. If you cannot do this exercise nine times, you may reduce the number to three times.

Change to your right foot and leg; the movements are the same as before (fig. 25). Also practice this nine times.

FIG. 25

CHAPTER 2
THE SECOND TECHNIQUE

Preparing Posture

Stand with your feet parallel and as wide apart as your shoulders (fig. 26). Smile inwardly and outwardly. Allow your body to be relaxed and tranquil, thinking nothing. Rotate your tongue inside your mouth. When there is saliva, swallow it to allow it to sink down to your "Dan Tian," an acupuncture point that is three fingers below your navel. Do this three times.

FIG. 26

Circling Palms

With your left leg and knee crossing in front of your right leg and knee, stretch your arms and hands forward much wider than your shoulders (fig. 27). The fingers and palms should face upward.

Then change, so your right leg and knee crosses your left leg and knee (fig. 28). Stretch your arms and hands forward much wider than your shoulders. Your fingers and palms face upward. Circle your fingers inward. The palms, arms, elbows,

FIG. 27

FIG. 28

FIG. 29

and wrists should also follow the movements.

Repeat these movements, left leg and right, nine times. If you find this too difficult to do when you first start doing these exercises, you may reduce the number to three times.

Next, cross your legs, putting your left leg over your right (fig. 29). Now your fingers and palms are facing downward, not upward. Circle the fingers inward, and your palms, arms, elbows, and wrists should follow the movements. Repeat this exercise nine times.

FIG. 30

Repeat this technique, but cross your right leg over the left. Your fingers and palms are still facing downward (fig. 30). Circle the fingers inward, and your palms, arms, elbows, and wrists should follow the movement (fig. 31). Repeat this exercise nine times.

FIG. 31

Both Palms Holding Heaven

Lift both your arms and hands up from the sides of your body (fig. 32). The palms should be facing upward and toward the front. Move them slowly and softly, raising them over your head. At the same time, the heels of the feet should slightly lift up off the ground, but the toes should be held firmly on the ground. Use your nose and your mouth to inhale deeply into your abdomen, in order to inhale fresh air and oxygen so that it will make the lower abdomen expand to its greatest extent.

FIG. 32

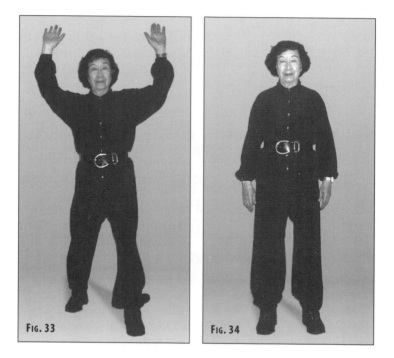

FIG. 33

FIG. 34

Lift your heels slightly off the ground (fig. 33). Then turn the palms to face downward, slowly dropping them down to your sides (fig. 34). Allow your heels to touch the ground as you exhale. Pull in your abdomen (concave). Slightly bending your knees, your upper body will follow a little bit forward. The diaphragm is moving up and down. The whole body is joining these movements. In this way, you can expel the stale air from your lungs, thus making your body healthy. Repeat these movements nine times. If you find this too difficult to do when you first start doing this exercise, you may reduce the number to three times.

Moving the Shoulders and Arms

You can use either of two methods for this exercise. The first method is easier; the second requires that you cross your legs and knees.

The first method: Stand with your feet parallel to each other and as wide apart as your shoulders. This exercise is very helpful for improving the activity of shoulder blades, chest, and arms. Your whole body should be relaxed. Slowly lift up your shoulders, following with your arms, elbows, wrists, and hands (fig.

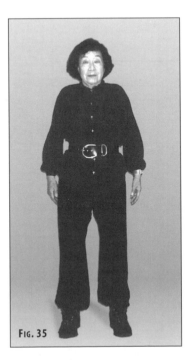

FIG. 35

35). Slowly raise them up. Then let them fall down. Repeat this exercise nine times.

Next use the shoulders to move your arms from the back to the front of your body, so that you extend your shoulder blades on both sides of your back. The backs of the hands also rotate opposite each other (fig. 36). By doing this, you dredge the meridian pathway of the back of the body. Then return shoulders, arms, and hands back to your original standing position. Then again move your shoulders and arms from back to the front of your body, extending the shoulder blades on your back. Repeat this exercise nine times.

Again, extend your chest while raising up your arms and hands; move them forward with palms upward (fig. 37).

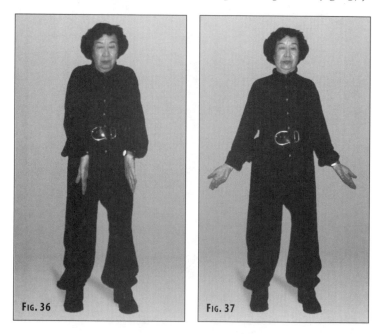

Fig. 36   Fig. 37

Contract your shoulder blades as much as you can. Your chest should be extended as much as possible. This exercise increases the activity of the lungs. Repeat this nine times.

The second method: With your right leg and knee crossing in front of your left leg and knee, slowly move the weight of your body to the back (left) foot. First, lift your shoulders up, then drop them down (fig. 38). Move the shoulders to bring your arms, elbows, and hands along. As you move them down, your left leg and knee will stimulate the calf of the right leg and knee, where there is an important acupuncture point named "Chengshan." Repeat these movements nine times.

FIG. 38

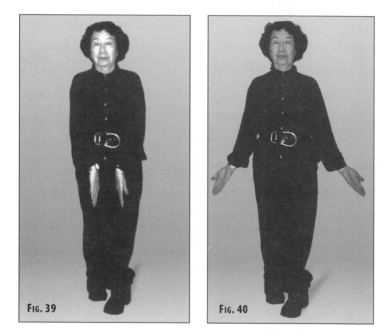

FIG. 39   FIG. 40

Second, cross your right leg and knee over your left leg and knee. Then move the shoulders from their outward position to the inward "shrugging" position (fig. 39). Your whole body should join in following these movements. Also be sure your left leg and knee stimulates the calf of the right leg, where there is the acupuncture point called "Chengshan." (See Diagram 1, page 14.) Repeat these movements nine times.

Third, extend your shoulders and palms from their inward to an outward position (fig. 40). When moving the shoulders, the whole body should be involved. The leg and knee are also moved as described above. Repeat these movements nine times.

Then change, letting your left leg and knee cross in front of your right leg and knee. Move your shoulders from their outward position to an inward "shrugging" position. Your whole body should be involved in these movements. Also be sure that your right leg and knee stimulates the calf of the left leg, stimulating the Chengshan acupuncture point. Repeat this exercise nine times.

You then extend your shoulders from an inward to an outward position. The leg and knee are moved to stimulate the Chengshan acupuncture point. Repeat nine times.

CHAPTER 3
THE THIRD TECHNIQUE

Preparing Posture

Stand with your feet parallel and as wide apart as your shoulders (fig. 41). Smile inwardly and outwardly. Allow your body to be relaxed and tranquil, thinking nothing. Rotate your tongue inside your mouth. When there is saliva, swallow it to allow it to sink down to your "Dan Tian," an acupuncture point that is three fingers below your navel. Do this three times.

FIG. 41

Playing the Lute

Take one step backward with your left foot. Lift up your left palm facing right with the fingers bending inward, as if you were holding something (fig. 42).

Fig. 42

Fig. 43

Then raise up your right hand and arm with the palm facing your left side. Move your palm to the left side (fig. 43), then move it back. Move it back and forth in front of your body, as if you were playing the lute. Do this several times.

Wind Blowing the Willow

Stand quietly, with your feet parallel and as wide apart as your shoulders. Relax your mind and muscles (fig. 44).

First, slightly bend your knees and twist your thighs and lower legs toward the left side of your body. Gently beat the right buttock with your right fist (fig. 45). The left fist rises up while you are doing this. There are two acupuncture points on your buttocks, one on each side of the body. The point is called "Huantiao." (See Diagram 2, page 40.) By gently beating your

FIG. 44

FIG. 45

buttocks, you can stimulate these points.

Then change; bend your knees and twist your thighs and lower legs toward the right side of your body, and beat your left buttock with your left fist (fig. 46). At the same time, your right fist rises up. As you beat your buttocks you again stimulate the "Huantiao" acupuncture point (see Diagram 2, page 40). Repeat these movements nine times. The effects of Wind Blowing the Willow will help eliminate pain in the lower back and buttocks region, muscular atro-

FIG. 46

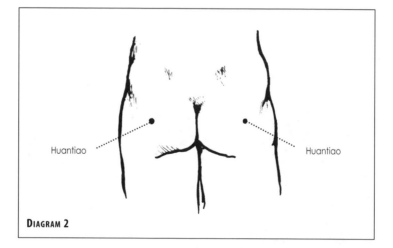

Huantiao   Huantiao

DIAGRAM 2

phy, motor impairment, pain and weakness of the lower extremities (hands and feet), and hemiplegia.

Mu Lan Pushing and Pulling the Loom

Mu Lan was known for her weaving. In order to develop these muscles, you need to do the following exercise. Stand quietly, with your feet parallel and as wide apart as your shoulders (fig. 47).

Raise up your hands and arms as if you were pushing the loom forward (fig. 48, on page 42); then pull it back (fig. 49).

FIG. 47

Lift up your left hand, and move your right hand as though you were throwing the shuttle of Mu Lan's loom from the right side to the left side (fig. 50). During this time, your eyes must follow the imaginary shuttle.

Then your hands and arms push the loom forward (fig. 51), and pull it back again (fig. 52).

With your left hand throwing the shuttle from the left side to the right side, allow your eyes to follow the shuttle. Move your lower legs and knees back and forth with your body as you weave. As you push and pull the loom forward and backward, it is best to let these movements synchronize with each other (fig. 53). The whole body and mind will be relaxed. Repeat these movements nine times.

FIG. 48

FIG. 49

FIG. 50

FIG. 51

FIG. 52

FIG. 53

Shrinking the Neck and Concaving the Abdomen

Keep your feet and thighs tightly together. Knees and ankle bones should also touch each other tightly. Draw your out-stretched fingers closely together and extend your arms down along the sides of your body, with your hands resting on your waist. Pull in your chin and smile both inwardly and outwardly (fig. 54)

FIG. 54

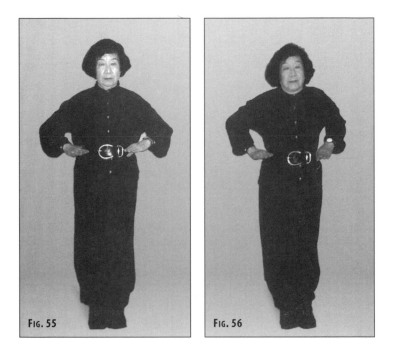

FIG. 55   FIG. 56

Then raise your hands and arms while bending them at the elbows and thrusting your elbows behind your body (fig. 55). Put your palms by the sides of your chest, the fingers close together and arms extended, with the palms facing down. Bend your knees slightly, while pulling your abdomen in tightly and shrinking your neck down into your shoulders (fig. 56).

Lower your body to a squatting position. As you do this, lift up your heels slightly, shifting your body weight onto the balls of the feet. This activates the Yongquan acupuncture point. (See Diagram 3.)

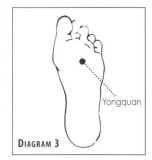

Yongquan

DIAGRAM 3

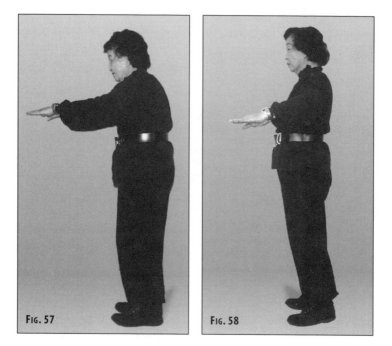

FIG. 57   FIG. 58

Stretch your hands and arms forward at chest level, and spread your hands outward (fig. 57), moving each of them out to trace a full circle. This "circle in the air" is done at "nipple level," with arms bent. Your hands come forward and the circle is done from the center outward. When you have traced a full circle, return your hands and arms to their place beside the chest.

While your hands and arms are making these circles, straighten your legs, thrust out your chest and abdomen, straighten your neck and stick out your hips. At the same time, slowly lower your heels down to the ground. This is a very subtle movement (fig. 58).

Now reverse the hand and arm movements so that the circles being described in the air go in the opposite direction. Stretch your hands and arms backward at the level of the solar plexus and spread them outward on either side (fig. 59), each time tracing a full circle from outside to inside, and each time returning your hands to their place alongside your chest.

Continue to do these hand and arm exercises as shown in the illustrations. Rotate your hands and arms from front to back nine times; then rotate your hands and arms in the reverse direction, from back to front, nine times. These movements are performed in the horizontal plane, level with the solar plexus (fig. 60).

FIG. 59   FIG. 60

The effects of this Shrinking Neck and Concaving Abdomen Kung will make your limbs more pliable. The exercise reduces your waist measurement, and helps you get rid of any extra weight you may be carrying. The motion of pulling the neck in and out is especially effective for preventing and alleviating dizziness, neck stiffness, tremors of the hands and head, neurasthenia, insomnia, and amnesia. Pulling the neck in and out also stimulates the thyroid gland, and it is helpful in reducing the size of an especially large, thick neck. If you have just recovered from a long illness and cannot do other kinds of exercises, this is an ideal kung to practice.

The Yongquan acupuncture point is located on the sole of the foot. The meridian energy moves up into the body from this acupuncture point, just as water springs from a fountain. It is a very important acupuncture point, and is called "the second heart" of the body. *Yong* means "gush out; well up," and *quan* means "spring," or "fountain."

CHAPTER 4

THE FOURTH TECHNIQUE

Preparing Posture

Stand with your feet parallel and as wide apart as your shoulders (fig. 61). Smile inwardly and outwardly. Allow your body to be relaxed and tranquil, thinking nothing. Rotate your tongue inside your mouth. When there is saliva, swallow it to allow it to sink down to your "Dan Tian," an acupuncture point that is three fingers below your navel. Do this three times.

FIG. 61

Mu Lan Combs Her Hair

With your left leg and knee crossing in front of your right leg and knee, slowly move your body toward the right, as low as you can. Raise up your left hand with an empty fist in front of your face, as if you are holding a mirror. With your right hand, gently "comb" the hair on your head from front to back (fig. 62). Do this nine times.

Then slowly stand up, change, and with your right leg and knee crossing in front of your left leg and knee, slowly move your

FIG. 62

FIG. 63

body toward the left side. Then slowly raise up the right fist in front of your face, as if you are holding a mirror. Lift up your left hand and gently "comb" your hair (fig. 63). Do this nine times. Then return to the beginning posture.

Mu Lan Washes the Thread and Puts It in the Sunshine

Bend your torso forward, raise your fists in front of your body—wider than your shoulders. Alternately, push your fists forward and pull them backward (fig. 64). One fist should be over the other. Your whole body will shake a little bit (fig. 65). Then hold your fists horizontally in front and by the sides of your body.

Move your fists horizontally from the left to right (fig. 66). Then lift them up (fig. 67) and allow them to fall down (fig. 68) again, from the right to left. Do this nine times.

Fig. 64   Fig. 65

Fig. 66

Fig. 67

Fig. 68

Pressing the Heels of the Palms

Hold your right arm by your side with the palm parallel to the ground. Your palm will be about thigh level. The left hand rests on your waist, with four fingers pointing toward the front and the thumb at the back, holding the waist. Bend your elbow and press the heel of your right palm at the right side of your body (fig. 69). Do this several times.

Then change. Put the heel of your left palm by your left side, while your right hand rests on your waist with its four fin-

FIG. 69

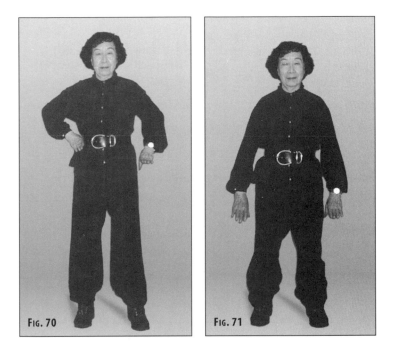

FIG. 70   FIG. 71

gers facing front and with the thumb back, holding the waist.
Bend your elbow and press the left heel of your left palm by your
left side, several times (fig. 70).

Next, perform these pressing movements with the heels of
both palms, pressing up and down by both sides of your body
(fig. 71). During this action, also begin to add another movement. You will start to slowly squat and then stand up. Do this
nine times.

Yin and Yang Palms

Stand quietly, with your feet parallel and as wide apart as your shoulders (fig. 72). Stretch your arms and hands out to both sides of your body. The left palm faces upward (signifying the Yang palm) and the right palm faces downward (signifying the Yin palm). As you stand firmly (fig. 73), slowly lift up your left leg and move your foot backward up and down nine times. If your physical condition won't allow you to do this nine times, you may do fewer times. You can begin to increase the number

FIG. 72

FIG. 73

FIG. 74

of times you do this as you feel more comfortable. You should not overtax your body.

Now it is time to change position. Raise your right leg and foot as though you were taking a step and leave your leg in mid-air, as shown in the illustration. Change your palms so that the right palm faces up, and the left palm faces down (fig. 74). Slowly lift your right foot backward up and down nine times.

CHAPTER 5

THE FIFTH TECHNIQUE

Preparing Posture

Stand with your feet parallel and as wide apart as your shoulders (fig. 75). Smile inwardly and outwardly. Allow your body to be relaxed and tranquil, thinking nothing. Rotate your tongue inside your mouth. When there is saliva, swallow it to allow it to sink down to your "Dan Tian," an acupuncture point that is three fingers below your navel. Do this three times.

FIG. 75

Returning the Body

First draw back your right foot. Then slowly and softly lift up your left arm and hand, palm facing down (fig. 76). While lifting up your arm, you should inhale.

Then slowly lower your arm, while you exhale (fig. 77). Again raise up and lower your arm while inhaling and exhaling. Repeat these movements nine times.

Return your right foot to a position parallel to your left foot. Now draw back your left foot. Slowly and softly lift up your

FIG. 76

FIG. 77

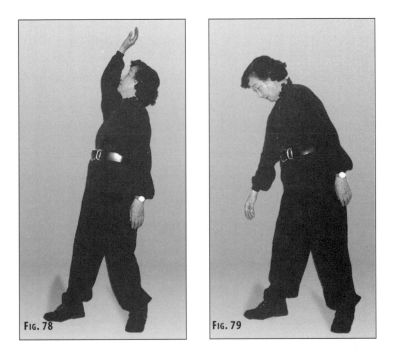

FIG. 78   FIG. 79

right arm and hand (fig. 78), and allow your arm to fall down again. As you lift up your arm and hand, inhale deeply.

As you lower your arm, slowly exhale (fig. 79). Repeat these movements nine times. At last, bring your left foot to the beginning position.

Rotating the Wheels

Stand quietly and relaxed, with your feet in a parallel position and as wide apart as your shoulders (Fig. 80).

Take half a step forward with your right foot. Lift up both fists from the sides of your body (fig. 81), fists facing each other. Rotate your fists alternately, in piston-like circular motions, with both fists moving forward and backward, up and down just like the pistons rotating in a steam engine. When your fists move forward and backward, your whole body also follows. (Here the

FIG. 80

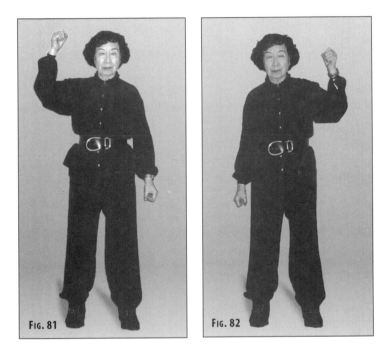

FIG. 81   FIG. 82

whole body means your legs, hips, waist, thighs, knees, lower legs, buttocks, calves, heels, and soles, including the shoulders.) As the fists are moving forward and backward, let your whole body join in these movements.

Then draw back your right foot so it is parallel to your left foot (fig. 82). Change, reverse the action, moving your left foot half a step forward. Do the same movements as described for the right foot. Repeat these movements nine times on each foot.

Rowing a Boat Against the Wind

Stand with your feet parallel and as wide apart as your shoulders (fig. 83).

Lift up both hands, as if you were holding a long oar in each hand (fig. 84). Move as if you were rowing a boat forward. Move your left foot forward one step and bend your leg and knee. Keep the right leg (in back) straight. At the same time bend your body forward a little bit. Move your arms and hands up and down, alternately rowing the boat, nine times.

FIG. 83

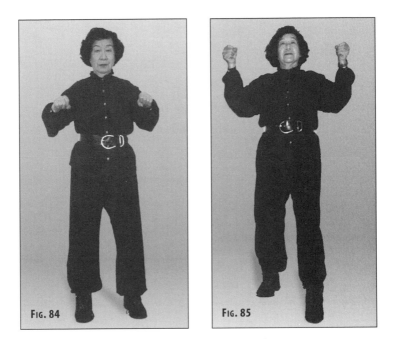

FIG. 84

FIG. 85

Now row the boat backward, with your empty fists facing upward, and pulling your arms back (fig. 85). Straighten the front foot and leg, and bend the back leg and foot. Rotate your arms and hands up and back, rowing the boat in this way nine times. Then return to the beginning posture.

Repeat the sequence, starting with your right foot forward one step, with bent leg.

Squatting and Touching the Fish

Stand in a relaxed and tranquil manner, with your feet as wide apart as your shoulders and parallel to each other. Cross your legs. Slowly squat as low as you can (fig. 86).

It will seem as if you are sitting. Stretch your palms forward, palms facing down. Imagine you are putting your fingers into the water to catch a fish (fig. 87).

Move both arms and hands from the left to the right (fig. 88), then from right to left. While moving, your body will bend

FIG. 86   FIG. 87

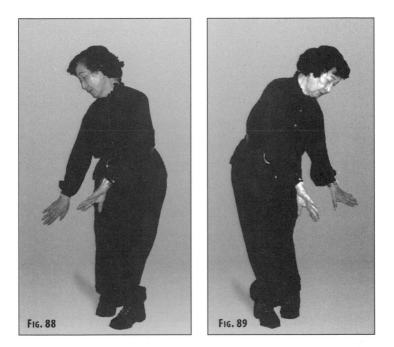

Fig. 88   Fig. 89

forward and your eyes will also follow your moving hands (fig. 89). Practice these movements nine times.

CHAPTER 6
THE SIXTH TECHNIQUE

Preparing Posture

Stand with your feet parallel and as wide apart as your shoulders (fig. 90). Smile inwardly and outwardly. Allow your body to be relaxed and tranquil, thinking nothing. Rotate your tongue inside your mouth. When there is saliva, swallow it to allow it to sink down to your "Dan Tian," an acupuncture point that is three fingers below your navel. Do this three times.

FIG. 90

Crossing Forearms

Step forward with your left foot. Lift up your left arm and hand, slowly and softly, over your head (fig. 91). Inhale deeply when you do this.

Then draw back your left foot so that both feet are parallel. Slowly bring down your left arm as you lift up your right arm and cross your forearms (the left forearm and the right forearm) in front of your body (fig. 92). Exhale. As you exhale, bend your body forward. Practice this nine times.

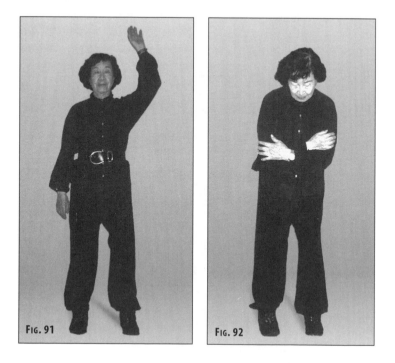

Fig. 91

Fig. 92

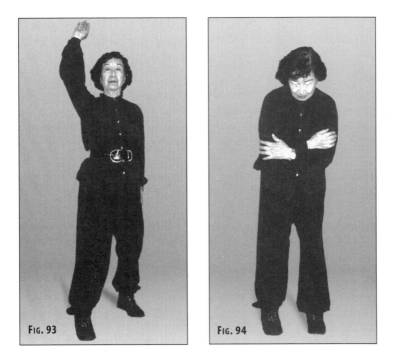

FIG. 93   FIG. 94

Change, and step forward with your right foot. Slowly lift up your right arm and hand over your head (fig. 93). Inhale deeply while you do this.

Bring down your right arm as you slowly raise your left forearm. Cross your forearms (right and left) in front of your body. Exhale, and as you are exhaling, bend your body forward slightly (fig. 94). Repeat these movements nine times.

Parting the Grass
and Searching

With your left leg and knee crossing over your right leg and knee, raise both palms in front of your body, so that the palms are facing each other in a position of prayer (fig. 95).

Then slowly rotate your palms, so that the backs of your hands nearly touch each other, so that the palms now face outward (fig. 96).

FIG. 95   **FIG. 96**

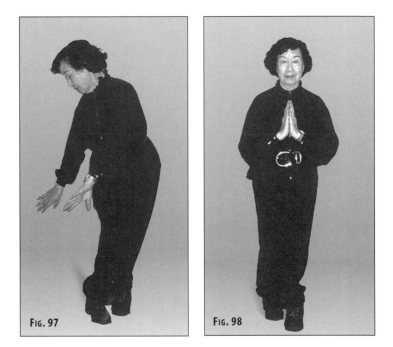

FIG. 97   FIG. 98

Slowly move your hands outward. At the same time look at the ground in front of you, as if you are parting the tall grass and searching for something (fig. 97). Then draw your hands back, rotating your palms and returning them to their original prayer position. Do this nine times.

Then change, so that your right leg and knee crosses over the left leg and knee. Raise both palms in front of your body, with the palms facing each other, as if you are praying (fig. 98).

FIG. 99 **FIG. 100**

Now rotate your palms so that the backs of your palms face each other. Then move them outward (fig. 99). Your eyes should be looking at the ground as if you are parting the tall grass and searching for something (fig. 100). Do this nine times.

Brushing the Knee
and Holding Heaven

Lift up your left foot and step forward. With your left hand, brush past your left knee. Push your right hand forward and rotate the palm upward (fig. 101).

Then turn the palm so that it faces up. Raise it up as high as you can. Imagine that you are holding the heavens up with your palm over your head (fig. 102). Place your weight on your left foot. The right heel is slightly raised off the ground. Slowly

FIG. 101   FIG. 102

FIG. 103   FIG. 104

move your left hand back and raise it behind your body. This will make your body balance itself. Do this nine times.

Now change, and with your right hand, brush your right knee and push your left hand forward with the palm facing upward (fig. 103). Rotate the palm facing up.

Slowly raise your hand up high over your head, as if you are holding up the heavens. Slowly move and raise your right hand behind your body (fig. 104). Do this nine times.

Crossing Legs and Shaking Shoulders

Place your left leg over the right leg, making contact with the knee and the "Chengshan" acupuncture point of the lower leg. (See Diagram 1, page 14.) Allow both shoulders to swing naturally back and forth. Gently squat and then stand up (fig. 105). When you do this "crossing legs" exercise, your knee will touch your calf. You will feel comfortable and when you shake your shoulders, your body moves so that when you squat and stand, your knee will touch your calf, thus stimulating the "Chengshan" acupuncture point.

Fig. 105

FIG. 106

Change positions so that your right leg crosses over your left leg, so that you make contact with the "Chengshan" acupuncture point. Allow both shoulders to swing back and forth naturally and gently at the sides of your body (fig. 106). Your whole body must be relaxed—not only the muscles, but also the mind. Slowly practice this nine times.

CHAPTER 7
THE SEVENTH TECHNIQUE

Preparing Posture

Stand with your feet parallel and as wide apart as your shoulders (fig. 107). Smile inwardly and outwardly. Allow your body to be relaxed and tranquil, thinking nothing. Rotate your tongue inside your mouth. When there is saliva, swallow it to allow it to sink down to your "Dan Tian," an acupuncture point that is three fingers below your navel. Do this three times.

Fig. 107

Touching the Cloud

Step forward with the left foot. Slowly raise up both hands, palms upward until they are parallel with the sides of your face (fig. 108). Then slowly rotate your palms until the four fingers of each hand are behind your ear, and the thumb is in front of your ear.

Lift both palms slowly over your head as high as you can. Turn the palms of both hands forward and upward. Imagine you are touching a cloud (fig. 109)

Fig. 108

Fig. 109

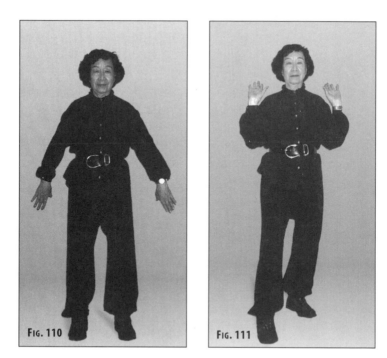

FIG. 110   FIG. 111

Slowly move your upper arms—with palms and fingers fac-ing down—to your sides. Hold your hands about waist level (fig. 110). Lift your palms slowly over your head and touch the cloud. Lower your palms again. Do this nine times.

With your right foot, take one step forward. Slowly raise up both hands, palms upward, to cheek level. Then slowly rotate your palms until the fingers are behind your ears. The thumbs will be in front of your ears (fig. 111).

Slowly lift up both hands over your head as high as you can (fig. 112, on page 90). Then turn the palms forward and upward. Imagine you are touching the cloud.

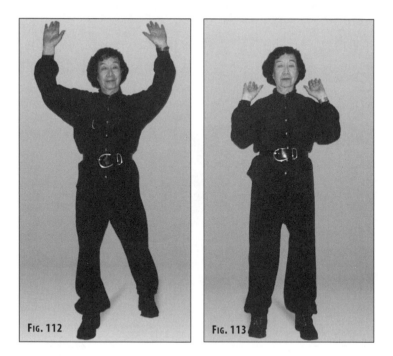

FIG. 112   FIG. 113

Slowly move your upper arms, with your palms and fingers facing down (fig. 113), down to your waist level. Repeat nine times.

Looking into the Well

Stand in a relaxed and tranquil way, with your feet parallel and as wide apart as your shoulders. Slowly raise up your arms and hands from back to front (fig. 114). Your head is between your two arms. Softly bend and let your body fall forward.

Then let the tips of your fingers touch the ground (fig. 115). The back, thighs, and lower legs must be kept straight. If you cannot do this, you may bend them a little bit. Repeat these movements nine times.

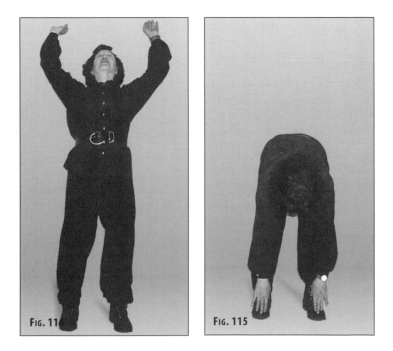

FIG. 114   FIG. 115

FIG. 116

Now stand as before. Slowly raise up your arms and hands above your head. Make sure that your head should be in the center, and your two arms reach over the head. While in this position, make your hands into fists. Slowly and softly bending forward, allow your hands (still forming fists) to touch the ground (fig. 116). Your back, thighs, and lower legs should be kept straight. This is a little bit more difficult than the first activity of touching the tips of the fingers to the ground. Repeat these movements nine times.

Swinging Hands

Stand with your feet parallel and shoulder-width apart. Smile inwardly and outwardly. Allow your body to relax while you do not think about anything (fig. 117).

This is one of the easiest of all kungs to perform. At least the movements themselves are extremely simple. Perhaps it will be more difficult to follow the instruction to "think of absolutely nothing" while you are doing this kung. Your mind should be

FIG. 117

Fig. 118

Fig. 119

completely empty, without a care in the world. Put yourself, as you prepare to begin this kung, into the state of mind of believing you are a weeping willow tree, with your limber branches being blown in the wind. Allow them to be blown in whatever direction the wind chooses to blow them. Allow the wind to direct your movements. Offer no resistance.

Your shoulders must be completely relaxed, with all tension and tightness gone. You are the supple willow tree being blown by the gentle spring breezes, swaying back and forth from left to right, then back again from right to left (Fig. 118).

When your body twists to the left side, the back of your left hand slaps your lower back, just below your waist (fig. 119).

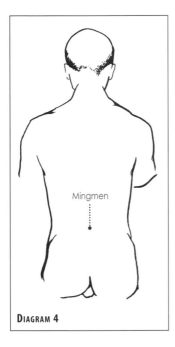

DIAGRAM 4

Mingmen is a very important acupuncture point. It is located in the middle of your lower back, exactly opposite your navel. It is the gate through which the vital chi energy moves in and out. This is the exact point at which your hand should make contact.

The palm faces outward. At the spot where your left hand touches, there is an acupuncture point named "Mingmen." (See Diagram 4.)

At the same time, the back of your right hand should be touching the front of your left shoulder, with the palm turned outward (fig. 120). When you twist your torso to the right side, the back of your

FIG. 120

right hand will touch your Mingmen, and the back of your left hand will touch your right shoulder.

Relax all the muscles, and, above all, relax your mind. Let go of all your thoughts. In this way, your body will become flex-ible. The chi (vital energy, or life force) and the blood will easily flow throughout your body. Repeat these movements nine times.

CHAPTER 8
THE EIGHTH TECHNIQUE

Preparing Posture

Stand with your feet parallel and as wide apart as your shoulders (fig. 121). Smile inwardly and outwardly. Allow your body to be relaxed and tranquil, thinking nothing. Rotate your tongue inside your mouth. When there is saliva, swallow it to allow it to sink down to your "Dan Tian," an acupuncture point that is three fingers below your navel. Do this three times.

FIG. 121

A Duck Walking into the Water

Slowly raise your arms and hands from your sides, with palms facing each other. Then rotate your palms so that the backs of your hands oppose each other (fig. 122). Slowly move your hands and arms from the front to the back of your body. During this time, turn your palms until the backs of both palms touch together to form a closing (fig. 123). Then the closed backs of your hands will rest on your lower back, just like the tail of a duck.

Fig. 122

FIG. 123

FIG. 124

FIG. 125

Happily walk into the water, lifting your right foot, and then letting your body "fall" down (fig. 124), with your whole body following and bending toward the right side, so that you are slightly squatting (fig. 125).

FIG. 126

Now walk to the left side. Lift up your left foot, then "fall down" with your whole body, following and bending, and squatting toward your left side (fig. 126). Walk for a while this way. Imagine that you are a duck walking happily into the water.

Shoulders Drawing Circles

Stand quietly, with your feet as far apart as the width of your shoulders. Shift the weight of your body onto the balls of your feet, and bend your knees slightly. Relax your whole body. Open your mouth slightly, in a natural way. Your arms should be facing down at your sides. Then rotate your shoulder joints alternately (fig. 127). To rotate your shoulders you should first lift up the left shoulder joint and rotate it toward the front, slowly moving upward.

FIG. 127

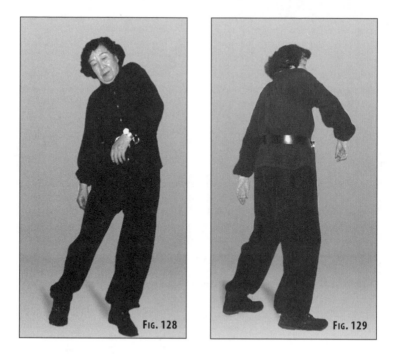

FIG. 128

FIG. 129

Then gradually move it backward and downward. Draw a circle with the left shoulder doing a round motion (fig. 128). Do this nine times.

During this time, your right shoulder is also moving from the back toward a downward rotating position, then forward and upward, also drawing a full circle (fig. 129). The motion of the shoulder joints should be allowed to move into your shoulders and you must bring your arms along as well. Do this nine times.

The continuous twisting of the upper part of your body squeezes (like a self-massage) the internal organs (fig. 130). The lungs can absorb oxygen and fresh air, you can also expel stale

FIG. 130 FIG. 131

(dirty) and waste chi (air) from your lungs (fig. 131). The func-
tion is that the internal organs can self-massage and also stimulate energy and blood circulation, thus reinforcing vitality and
helping to cure chronic diseases. Do this nine times.

Looking into the Water

Stand in a tranquil and relaxed way. Cross your right leg and knee over your left leg and knee. Raise your hands and arms to frame the sides of your face. Your hands and palms should face inward (fig. 132). Slowly move your body toward the right in an arc, bending your torso low. Your eyes should pretend to look at the water, as if the water were a mirror. Do this nine times.

Fig. 132

Now stand up. Change position so that now your left leg and knee cross over the right leg and knee (fig. 133). Bring your palms to your cheek level. Slowly move your torso toward the left. Then look into the water, as if you were looking into a mirror (fig. 134). Do this nine times.

Five Fingers Quarrel

Once upon a time the fingers discussed which was the best one among them, because they wanted to choose who was the most important.

First of all, the thumb said, "I am the best among us," but the others did not agree with his opinion. The thumb argued with them. He said, "Both now and in the past, whenever any person, rich or poor, wants to show that something wonderful has happened in their lives, he or she always sticks up their thumb to show victory, and to convince everyone else it was really a miracle." The other fingers were not convinced.

Next, the index finger said, "People eat every day. Whenever the cooks need to test the food, to see if it is sweet or salty, they must use me to taste it. Because I am so useful, I must be the best." This didn't end the argument.

Then the middle finger spoke: "I am the longest one among us; all of you are shorter than I. This is the truth, you can't argue with me. I keep the truth." But the other fingers argued with him anyway.

It was the ring-finger's turn: "I am very proud. Any person who has a ring, whether it is silver or gold, jade or precious stone, for engagement or wedding, always wears his or ring on me. I always get to show a person's pride, so I must be the best." There was still no agreement.

Finally, the last one, the little finger, spoke up: "I am the last one, and I am smaller than all of you. But I am very lucky and very proud. Perhaps you don't know why; let me tell you. Any time, any place in the world, wherever you go, when people go to a temple or church to worship, whether Buddha, Allah, Tao, or God, they always press their palms together to make prayers. When they do, I am the closest to god." And that ended the argument.

Glossary of Terms

Baihui. The point at the top of the head; the crown.

Changqiang. The point located on the coccyx or tail bone; the starting point of the Du Channel.

Chengjiang. Point in the middle of the depression between lower lip and chin.

Chengshan. The acupuncture point located on the back of each calf. Benefits: it can help to cure lower back pain, constipation, spasm of the gastrocnemius, and hemorrhoids.

Daimai. Belt Channel, waistline; begins under the navel, where it divides into two branches which extend around the waist to the small of the back.

Dan Tian. A point three fingers below the navel. This point can be called the "sea" for the chi of the whole body.

Deimei. See *Daimai*.

Dumai. Du Channel—runs along the spinal column from the Changqiang, the neck, to the skull, over the crown of the head to the roof of the mouth. This channel is very strong, connecting the nervous system of the body. It passes through 28 acupuncture points located mostly along the spine.

Empty Fists. Fingers naturally close together with the thumb touching the tip of the middle (long) finger. Palms are empty.

Huantiao. This acupuncture point is located on both buttocks. Indications: pain in the lower back and hip region, pain and weakness of the lower extremities, and hemiplegia.

Huiyin. Perineum; the point between the anus and the genital organ.

Joyu. The region of the kidneys.

Laogong. The point near the center of the palm (Inside Laogong); Outside Laogong is located in the center of the back of the hand. "Lao" equals "work, labor"; "Gong" equals palace. This point is very important in the treatment of diseases.

Mingmen. The point on the lower back, opposite the navel. This is a very important point through which the vital energy of life goes in and out; it is a gate.

Renmai. Ren Channel—goes through the center and front of the body. It begins at the perineum and extends up to the base of the mouth. When the tongue rests against the palate, it forms a bridge between dumai and renmai. This channel has 24 acupuncture points.

Shenyu. These two points are located on both sides of the ming-men. They store up water for the proper functioning of the kidneys.

Tianmu. A point between the eyebrows, just below the center of the forehead; also referred to as the "Third Eye." It is the point of clarity.

Yingtan. The point located above and between the eyebrows. This is where chi enters the head to benefit the brain.

ACUPUNCTURE POINTS
AND ENERGY CHANNELS

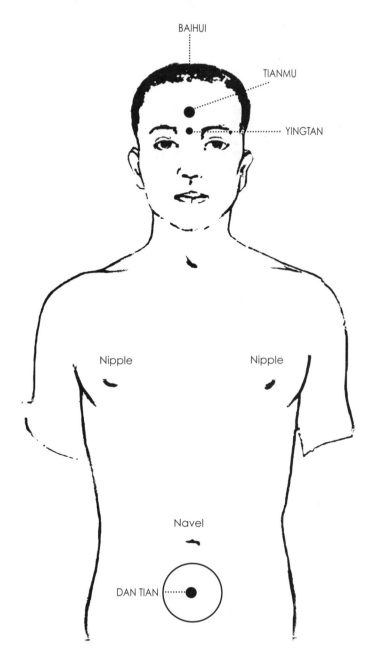

Dan Tian and the Major Acupuncture Points

In descending order from the top of the skull:

Baihui: At the top of the head; crown.

Tianmu: Between the eyebrows, just below the center of the forehead. The "Third Eye."

Yingtan: Between the eyebrows.

Dan Tian: The point three fingers width below the navel.

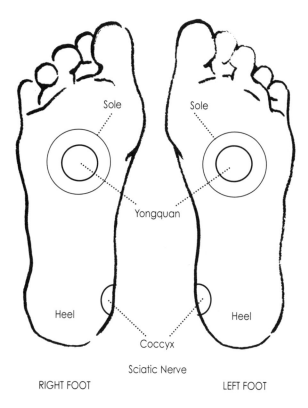

The feet, the roots of the body. Feet are the reflexes of the body's organs, glands, and limbs.

1

Baihui

This point is at the top of
the head.

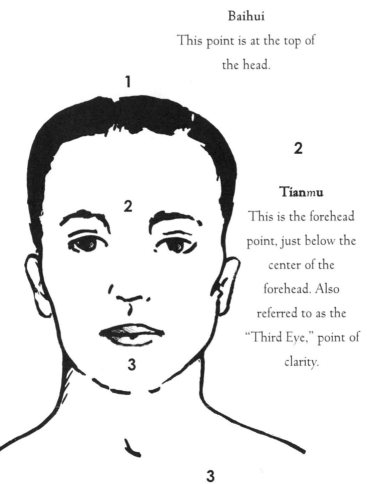

2

Tianmu

This is the forehead
point, just below the
center of the
forehead. Also
referred to as the
"Third Eye," point of
clarity.

3

Chengjiang

This point is in the middle of the
depression between the lower lip and
the chin. Saliva collects at this point.

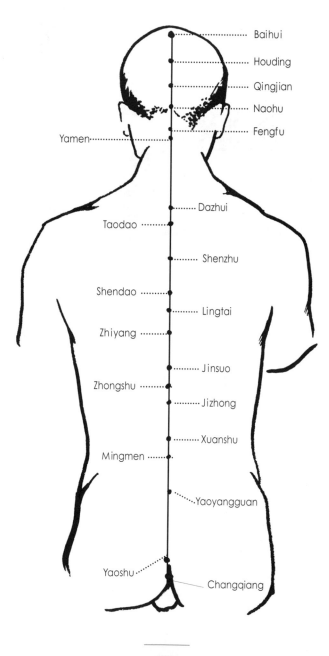

Baihui
Houding
Qingjian
Naohu
Fengfu
Yamen
Dazhui
Taodao
Shenzhu
Shendao
Lingtai
Zhiyang
Jinsuo
Zhongshu
Jizhong
Xuanshu
Mingmen
Yaoyangguan
Yaoshu
Changqiang

Du Mai (Du Channel)

This is a channel that begins at Changqiang. This channel is very strong, connecting the nervous system of the body. It passes through 28 acupuncture points located mostly along the spine. At the nape of the neck (or back), this channel enters the brain, moving through Baihui, around on the forehead and ending at a point at the front of the hard palate (roof of the mouth).

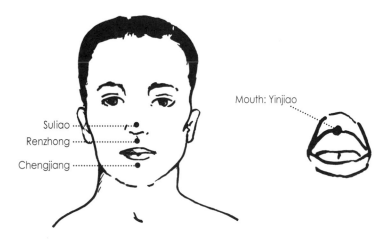

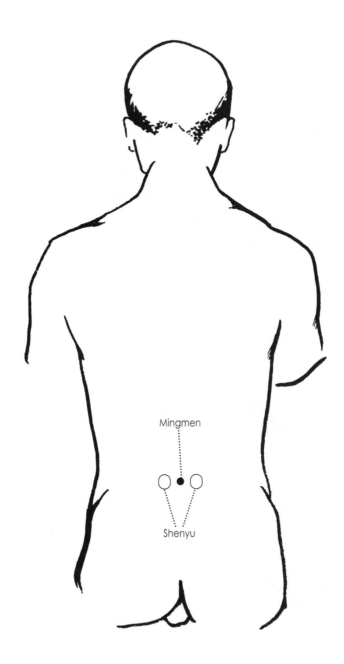

Mingmen

This point is in the lower back opposite the navel. This is a very important point through which the vital energy of life goes in and out; it is a gate.

Shenyu

These two points are located on each side of the Mingmen. These points store up water for the proper functioning of the kidneys.

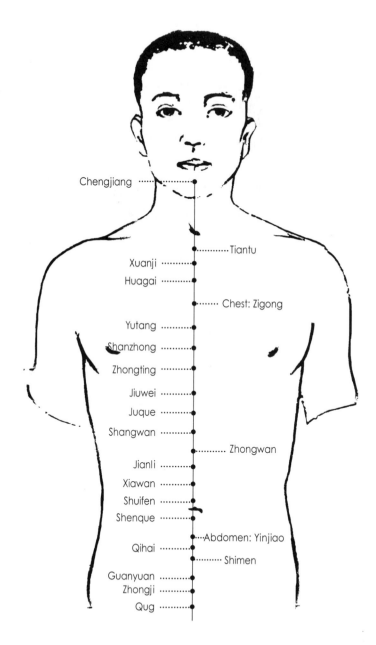

Chengjiang

Tiantu

Xuanji

Huagai

Chest: Zigong

Yutang

Shanzhong

Zhongting

Jiuwei

Juque

Shangwan

Zhongwan

Jianli

Xiawan

Shuifen

Shenque

Abdomen: Yinjiao

Qihai

Shimen

Guanyuan

Zhongji

Qug

Ren Mai (Ren Channel)

The Ren Channel arises from the lower abdomen and emerges from the perineum. It ascends along the interior of the abdomen, and the front midline to the throat, up to the Chengjiang. The Ren Channel has 24 points.

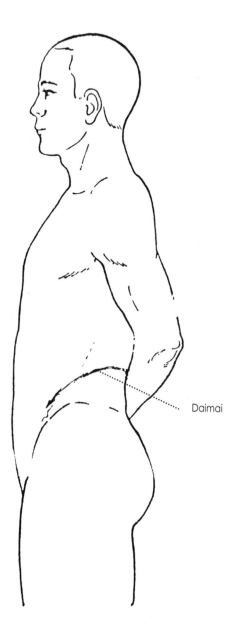

Daimai

Daimai

This is the line or meridian that circles the waist. "Holy Wheel Rotating Forever" dredges into the channel of Dai Mai.

Huantiao

This acupuncture point is located on both buttocks. Indications: pain in the lower back and hip region, pain and weakness of the lower extremities and hemiplegia.

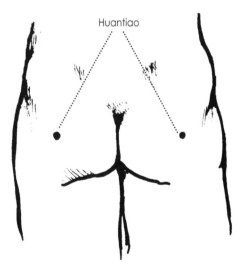

Huiyin

This point is at the lowest part of the abdomen. It is a place where Yin energy gathers and three meridians—the Ren Channel, Du Channel, and Chong (Vital) Channel—meet together. It is a very important point. It is in the center of the perineum, between the anus and the scrotum in males and between the anus and the posterior labial commissure in females.

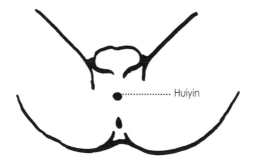

Chengshan

The acupuncture point located on the back of each calf. Benefits: it can help to cure lower back pain, constipation, spasm of the gastrocnemius, and hemorrhoids.

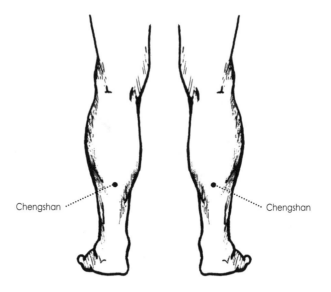

Chengshan .... Chengshan

Yongquan

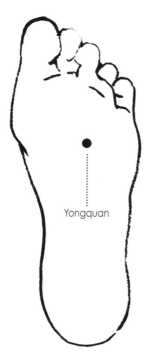

Yongquan

This acupuncture point is on the sole of the foot. The meridian energy moves up into the body from this acupuncture point, just as water springs from a fountain. This acupuncture point is very important, and it is considered as a second heart in Traditional Chinese Medicine.

APPENDIX 2

TESTIMONIALS

JULY 21, 1995

Mu Lan Chuan;

After my first lesson I felt happy and energized, more energy than before. This lightness of mood encourages me to practice every day.

I eagerly look forward to another lesson. The movements are graceful and simple. Professor Sheng is a patient and exacting teacher.

Thank you,

Linda Kay Deaton, RN

AUGUST 10, 1995

Today I felt achy and out of sorts, disconnected. After practicing Mu Lan Chuan for one hour with Professor Sheng, my body feels energized. My back no longer aches. My mind is clear, like a pool of water undisturbed. My energy opens and feels connected.

We practiced the first part and learned the second part. The squatting is hard work but it makes the body feel limber and active. There is no residual soreness, only a sense of strengthening and energy.

Thank you,

Linda Kay Deaton, RN

AUGUST 10, 1995

Today I learned several new Mu Lan Chuan movements. I feel more energized and relaxed. I look forward to each class time. I try to practice Mu Lan Chuan each day. The result of this practice, especially using the deep breathing movements just prior to bedtime, has lessened my insomnia. I'm sleeping better at night. I'm now not taking any medication to sleep.

Thank you,

Ruth A. Riad

AUGUST 31, 1995

Today after doing Mu Lan Chuan I could feel energy move through the left side of my body. After massaging my "chengshan" point, my knees felt very warm. On right side of body my muscle was very tense and burning. I could feel this during the class time. Following Mu Lan Chuan movements during rest time still some burning. My mind feels very relaxed. It's important to spend a few minutes to let go of all issues and take care of yourself.

Thank you,

Ruth A. Riad

AUGUST 5, 1995

I have been doing Tai Chi Chuan for ten years, so movements are familiar—soft, easy, extended motions within the body. Today I experienced Mu Lan Chuan from Professor Sheng, who has directed the lessons very well. I feel the "chi" energy moving strongly throughout my body and limbs. It is very powerful work—benefitting the total system. It is a wonderful experience.

Thank you—many thanks for the lesson.

Robert Lew

AUGUST 5, 1995

I had practiced Chi Kung several years ago and lost weight. Unfortunately, I did not continue to practice and found my health and weight a problem again. Now as I study Mu Lan Chuan I am feeling increasing energy. I have been surprised at how difficult the movements have been for me. This makes me more aware of how much Chi Kung increases stamina and general well-being. I am also starting to lose weight again and hope to regain both health and vitality.

Thank you Professor Sheng.

Gina Vaughn

Before I met Professor Sheng, my job as a teacher was leaving me stressed and fatigued at the end of a day. I had gained a lot of weight and did not feel healthy or energetic. I was looking for a form of exercise which would help me to restore both. Professor Sheng introduced me to Ch'i Kung through the form Shin Shen Tsuan Kung. She taught me to practice this form. Focus on relaxation, and the movement of ch'i along the meridians, I began to feel a dramatic change taking place in my health and energy level. Later I learned the Flying Crane Ch'i Kung and part of Ru

Yu Tai Ch'i. Now as I practice Ch'i Kung, I notice an increase of energy that allows me to go through an entire day of teaching and leave work energized rather than fatigued. I find myself able to draw on energy resources I did not know I had.

I also have noticed a growing rejection of heavy and junk food by my body which is now signalling it wishes to be lighter and more energetic.

I am beginning to sense Ch'i as a form of universal energy which enters my body, then flows back out again to the universe.

This has led to an increasing feeling of being at one with Nature and Nature's consciousness. I love the feeling of being at home in the wind, sunshine, the clouds and rain, deriving and giving back the energy of all life.

Thank you for furthering my quest for this understanding.

Gina Vaughn

MAY 22, 1995.

Mu Lan Chuan:

Today I learned Mu Lan Chuan from Professor Sheng. This is my first encounter with this kung. The posture is very different from other kungs.

The stimulation is immediate, especially below the knees, and when I raise my arms the energy is very strong.

This kung is very positive and energizing.

Julia Morin-Wisner

JUNE 19, 1995

Mu Lan Chuan:

This is the third lesson Mu Lan Chuan from Professor Sheng.

I feel the energy in different ways. First the energy goes up and down my body. I can breathe very easy and full.

Then the energy is from side to side, through my hands and across my chest.

I feel very energized and "up-feeling" and a lot of warmth throughout.

The warm feeling slowly descends as I am coming to the close of my lesson.

Julia Morin-Wisner

JULY 17, 1995

Practicing Mu Lan Chuan with Professor Sheng.

After fifteen minutes I started sweating and felt very energized all over my body. I felt the acupressure point, "Holding up the Mountain," releasing a lot of energy. After the class I felt warm and energized.

Thank you Professor Sheng.

Monika Fimpel

Index